# Alphabet Bandits

## An ABC Book

BY MARCIA LEONARD
PICTURES BY MARYANN COCCA-LEFFLER

**Troll Associates**

Library of Congress Cataloging-in-Publication Data

Leonard, Marcia.
   Alphabet bandits: an ABC book / by Marcia Leonard; pictures by
Maryann Cocca-Leffler.
      p.    cm.
   Summary: The Raccoon Bandits learn the alphabet by taking letters
from a variety of foods.
   ISBN 0-8167-1718-4 (lib. bdg.)        ISBN 0-8167-1719-2 (pbk.)
   [1. Alphabet.   2. Food—Fiction.   3. Raccoons—Fiction.]
I. Cocca-Leffler, Maryann, 1958-      ill.   II. Title.
PZ7.L549Al   1990
[E]—dc20                                                89-4933

The Bandits wanted an alphabet
so they could learn
all the letters from A to Z.

**Aa**

They took an **A** from Apple

**Bb**

Banana

and a **B** from Banana,

# Cc

C<sub>ookie</sub>

a **C** from Cookie

**Dd**

Doughnut

and a **D** from Doughnut.

# Ee

Eclair

Frosting

# Ff

They found an E and an F
in an Eclair with Frosting.

**G**ingerbread man

**Gg**

And they got a **G** from a Gingerbread man.

"This is a good start," said the Bandits. "But let's keep looking."

# Hh

Hamburger

They discovered an **H** in Hamburger,

# Ii

an **I** in Ice cubes, and a **J** in Juice.

# Jj

# Kk

**K**iwi fruit

**L**imes
and
Lemons

# Ll

They grabbed a **K** from Kiwi fruit
and an **L** from Limes and Lemons.

# Mm

Macaroni

Then they picked up an **M** from Macaroni.

# Nn

"More letters!" said the Bandits.
"We still need more letters."

Nuts

Quickly they collected an **N** from Nuts,

**Oo**

an **O** from Olives, and a **P** from Pickles.

**Pp**

# Qq

**Q**uart

**R**aspberries

# Rr

Then they gathered a **Q** and an **R**
from a Quart of Raspberries,

**Ss**

**S**paghetti

**T**omato sauce

**Tt**

and they forked up an **S** and a **T**
from Spaghetti with Tomato sauce.

# Uu

Upside-down cake

Vanilla ice cream

# Vv

"Just a few more letters," said the Bandits.
"Then we'll have them all."

They scooped up a **U** and a **V** from
Upside-down cake with Vanilla ice cream.

# Ww

**W**atermelon

e**X**tra sweet

# Xx

Then they took a **W** and an **X** from
a Watermelon that was eXtra sweet.

# Yy

Yogurt

And finally they got a **Y** from Yogurt

**Zz**

Zucchini

and a **Z** from Zucchini.

By the time they finished their alphabet,
the Bandits had learned all the
letters from A to Z.

And they were very, very full.